Another Girl Calls My Dad Daddy

Emma L. Price

Another Girl Calls My Dad Daddy

Emma L. Price

ELPBooks
California

Copyright © 2014 by Emma L. Price
ISBN 13: 987-0-9841650-2-5
ISBN 10: 0-9841650-2-9

Library of Congress Number: 2914919055
Printed in the United States of America
First Printing 2015

10 9 8 7 6 5 4 3 2 1
www.elpbooks.net

Interior Designer – John Sibley – Rock Solid Production

Summary: Twelve-year-old Portia Maddox couldn't wait to meet her older half-sister, but when she finally met her, it wasn't what she had expected.

[1. Type 1 Diabetes—Fiction
2. Sibling Rivalry—Fiction   3. Family—Fiction
4. Bullying—Fiction   5. Artificial Pancreas—Fact]

Dedication

This book is dedicated to those who braved diabetes, to the families and friends who love them, my mother who died from the many complications of diabetes and especially the young people I know who have type 1 diabetes.

Another Girl Calls My Dad Daddy is also dedicated to the little ones in my family who loves to read; Dejah, Marlon, Aireana and DJ.

You can't control the wind.
But you can adjust your sail.
—Anonymous

Chapter One

My heart was racing. *Thump. Thump. Thump. Thump.*

"Do you think she'll like me?" I asked for the umpteenth time.

"She'll like you," Dad answered. "You two got along well over the phone this year, didn't you?"

I checked my watch. Ten more minutes and our plane would land.

"Yes, but for the past three weeks I haven't heard from her. The two times we talked this month, our calls were really short, and I did most of the talking. Maybe I said something to make her mad."

I grabbed Dad's hand. It was sweaty like mine. Our eyes locked. I think he was more nervous than I was.

"What time is it?"

Dad smiled. "My watch has the same time as yours."

He playfully pushed in my nose. "Before we left home you made sure our watches had the same time."

Last summer, my parents had told me I had a fifteen-year-old half-sister. I thought that was so cool. Dad wanted us to get to know each other. He said enough time had been lost. She lives in another state with her mother. He called Jasmine, my half-sister, and introduced us, and we hit it off. We couldn't talk during the week because of school, but on Saturday mornings Dad didn't mind that I called her or how long we talked.

"Portia, call me 'Jazz' like my other friends," Jasmine said during one of our first chitchats. That made me like her even more.

"Glad I'm no longer an only child," I sang into the receiver while we were yakking at another time.

"Yeah. You are my baby sister, and I like that." Jasmine giggled on the other end.

Sometimes when we talked, I didn't want to hang up. I'd say, "Jazz, you hang up first." And Jasmine would say, "No, you hang up first." Then we'd start talking and laughing about one of our favorite TV shows.

"Do you think she'll like the necklace I made for her at camp last summer?" I had it in my tote bag.

"Sure she will. Most people like unexpected gifts," he said. "And you know she said she loves jewelry just like you."

I had been on cloud nine since my parents had decided that Jasmine could come spend three weeks with us. I had begged Dad to let me fly with him to get her.

"Why didn't you know about Jasmine when she was a baby?" I asked.

"You remember, last summer I told you that Jasmine's mother and I got married our first year in college. After college, couldn't find a job, so I joined the Air Force. After I'd gone off to basic training, Vivian's father got sick, and she went back to her home to take care of him." Dad closed the book that he had been reading. "About six months later, she sent divorce papers and asked me to sign them. I tried to talk her out of getting a divorce, but she said we'd gotten married too young, and we really didn't know each other. I finally signed the papers. She never told me we were going to be parents. Three years later, I got out of the Air Force, met your mom, fell in love, and we got married. Jasmine was fourteen years old before Vivian finally told me about her."

"Do you think Jasmine is mad at you because you've

never been to see her?"

"Well, Jasmine sounds like a mature young lady. I'm sure she wishes things had been different, but I don't think she's angry. Vivian told her what happened, so she knows I didn't abandon her."

"I want her to like us and have fun at our house," I said, listening to the wind outside the plane.

"Me too," Dad said.

"Last month, after I told Jasmine that you and her mother said she could come for a visit when school ended, she wasn't as talkative and funny as before. She didn't call me the next weekend like she'd said she would and when I called her, Vivian said she was out with friends. Something must have happened."

Butterflies are dancing in my stomach.

"I don't know why she didn't want to talk much after I told her we were coming to get her. Do you think Vivian is making her come?"

"Don't know, Baby. Maybe she is nervous, too. We'll have to wait 'til we get there and see," Dad answered.

"How long will it take to get from the airport to her apartment?" I asked.

"Not sure," Dad said. "I think it's about an hour's

drive. We're going to check into the hotel first. I know you're anxious to see Jasmine, but we'll make it quick."

Check into the hotel and an hour's drive—that's too long.

I had just begun to relax when the flight attendant announced, "Ladies and gentlemen, we've reached our final destination. Thank you for flying with us. Please come back to see us real soon."

Dad's hand gripped mine a little tighter as we stepped off the plane and headed to get our bags.

Dad had promised to make it quick, but it took forever to pick up our luggage, get a rental car and check into the hotel. Finally, we headed off to meet Jasmine.

"I'm scared. What if we have nothing to talk about?"

"Just talk about the same things you did on the phone," Dad said, with a chuckle.

But I was worried. I didn't want to make any mistakes. I wanted her to like me.

Dad pulled into a wide driveway and parked the car in a spot marked "Guest." We got out, walked to the entrance and found apartment number twelve. He stood back and let me ring the doorbell.

I was shaking. The palms of my hands were sweaty.

Jasmine opened the door and stepped out in front of me.

"Hey, Baby Sister," she said. "Glad to meet you."

Hazel eyes, just like mine, flashed at me through gobs of thick black mascara.

She didn't look anything like the pictures she'd sent me.

Something was wrong.

Chapter Two

Jasmine pulled me into her arms and gave me a tight squeeze. I hugged her back. "I'm glad to meet you, too," I said.

Dad stepped beside me.

Jasmine turned to face him. "Oooh, thanks for coming to get me, Daddy."

I felt like I had been punched in the stomach. Now beads of sweat rolled down my forehead.

Oh, boy! I'll have to get used to her calling him Daddy. He *is* her father, too.

Jasmine gave Dad a long hug.

"Baby, it's my pleasure. You don't know how long I've wanted to see you." Dad sounded like he was apologizing.

I knew I was going to have to share Dad. I was happy and didn't want this moment to end. So I pushed back my selfish feelings.

Jasmine's amber skin glowed in the sunlight. It was the same shade as our father. She wore an avocado-green halter top, and her stomach poked out over the waistband of a multicolored mini-skirt like a cinnamon muffin. Her long gold earrings nearly touched her shoulders.

Dad's eyes sparkled, and he chuckled, "Jasmine, Portia couldn't wait to come get you."

"Jasmine?" called a soft voice from behind the door. "Who's there?"

"It's Daddy," she sang. "And Portia." She flashed a wide grin my way.

Jasmine beamed and grabbed our hands. "Let's go inside."

A tall, thin lady threw her arms around Dad and gave him a quick hug. Turning to me, she said, "And you must be Portia."

I smiled.

She examined me from head to toe. "I'm Vivian. You and Jasmine *could* pass for twins."

Jasmine had sent me pictures, and my friends said we looked alike, too.

I glanced at her. She didn't look like the Jasmine in

the pictures. She hadn't worn any makeup or earrings in the pictures, and she had been much thinner. Now she had on way too much makeup and there was a frown on her face.

"Come in, you two, and get comfortable. I hope you're hungry, because you're just in time for dinner."

Yummy! It smells like meatloaf, but whatever it is, I'm in.

"That's nice of you, Vivian," Dad said. "We don't want to be a bother. We're only going to stay one night. I have to work day after tomorrow. I couldn't take any extra time off right now. Portia wouldn't let me rest until I came for Jasmine, so we took an early flight this morning." He smiled and winked at me. "Right, Baby?"

"Really, Portia?" Jasmine said. "You couldn't wait to come get me?"

Is Jasmine taunting me? No, I'm reading too much into this.

I was so nervous I couldn't think of anything to say, so I raised my eyebrows and glanced at Dad.

He smiled. "Yes, she's excited to have a big sister, and we're both glad you're coming home with us. Grace is, too"

"Going to be lonely without Jasmine," Vivian said

with a sigh. She looked at her and smiled. "But, I'm happy you and Grace invited her to visit this summer. She really needs this."

Jasmine let out a loud groan and anxiously tucked a few stray brown curls behind her ear. "Let's go wash for dinner, Portia."

She led the way to the bathroom, and I went in first. A small tattered rug lay on the floor in front of the sink, and a torn green bath towel hung beside the face bowl on a crooked rack. It was hard turning on the hot water faucet, and water gushed out of the cold one too fast. I had to jump back so it wouldn't splash on me.

I needed to test my blood sugar, but I couldn't let Jasmine know about my diabetes yet. All those times we had talked on the phone, I had never told her. I had wanted to wait until we were face to face. Although it's been four years since I was diagnosed, I still don't like anyone to know I have type 1 diabetes.

I felt her eyes staring at me. I quickly dried my hands and stepped aside.

"You're skinny," she hissed in my face when I turned around. "I can almost see through you. You look like a little stick." Her hot breath burned my cheeks, and I stepped back out of her way.

It had taken three years to accept that I was thinner than most of my friends who were the same age as me. Ever since I had been diagnosed with type 1 diabetes, I had been self-conscious about my size. No matter how much I ate, I couldn't gain one ounce. When I turned twelve, I'd accepted being thin, but now Jasmine's words brought back all those old hurtful feelings.

She frowned and leaned in closer. "I'm going to call you Miss Skinny Minny," she whispered.

"Why are you calling me names? You were so nice over the phone. What's happened to you?"

Jasmine brushed past me and jeered, "That was *before* I saw you and how *he* treats you! Just like royalty. I don't like 'daddy's little girls,' and you're such a sweet little princess, aren't you?"

I might be small for my age but I'm not a little girl, and I don't let people push me around.

"Jazz, why are you acting like this? Ever since Daddy told me about you, I've been dying to meet you. I loved talking with you on the phone all those times. You were nice and funny. What's wrong?"

"Don't *you* call me Jazz. Only the people I like call

me that."

That really hurt.

Jasmine bent over to wash her hands.

My insulin pod beeped. I nearly fainted. Did she hear it?

"What's that noise?" she asked, turning to face me.

"It's my watch letting me know it's time to eat."

"See, you *are* a big baby, if you need a watch to tell you when to eat. You're spoiled, too. Rotten. I can see you have Daddy wrapped around your little finger." Jasmine turned back to the sink. "Me, I have to fight for everything I get." The water splashed into the sink and she said, "Anyway, why did you want to meet me? You have it all."

I was glad she forgot about the beeping, but I wanted her to know how happy I was that she was coming with us.

"You're Daddy's daughter and my big sister. Don't you want to get to know us?"

Jasmine looked at herself in the mirror, pulled back a few curls and touched her earrings.

"Why should I? Our daddy divorced my mom before I was born." Her voice quivered as she spun around and faced me. "He doesn't care about me! Sixteen years and this is the first time I've seen him. And you, Miss Goody-Goody, have had the best all your life."

"That's not true. Daddy does care about you. When he found out that he had another daughter, he wanted to come see you. Your mother told him no and that you would be confused. After that, he told Mom about you and then told me. He kept on asking your mom to let him see you. Didn't your mom tell you that?"

She rubbed the bar of soap between her hands as fast as she could.

"Mom said a lot of things, but I don't believe her. Besides, she didn't say anything about him until I pressured her. All she cares about is how much I eat, who I hang out with, and now she wants to ship me away to live with you guys so she can be with her friends." Jasmine shut off the water. "She doesn't have time for me anymore." She turned and angrily flung her wet hands at me.

Water splashed on the front of my new blouse. I jumped back. "What are you doing?"

Wiping her hands, she narrowed her eyes. "Sorry, it was an accident. I was reaching for the towel," she said, flouncing out of the bathroom.

"Hey, Jasmine, my blouse is sopped," I called after her.

I couldn't believe she had done that, and she wasn't sorry. That was just plain spiteful. What was the matter with her?

Fuming, I followed her to the kitchen.

Dad and Vivian were sitting at the table talking in low voices. They looked up and smiled when we walked in.

Chapter Three

I eased into the chair with my arms crossed, attempting to hide the wet top. It clung to me, and I kept trying to pull it away from my skin.

Jasmine flopped down in her chair, smirking while piling mashed potatoes, gravy and a huge piece of meatloaf on her plate.

Vivian's eyes focused on my soaked blouse. "Jasmine, what happened to Portia?"

I didn't want to get Jasmine in trouble. I wanted her to come home with us. If Vivian raised a stink, Jasmine might change her mind. I sat silently, eyes down on my plate, and didn't say a word.

"Don't blame me!" Jasmine huffed. I could feel her eyes glaring at me. "Portia just turned on the water too fast."

Dad rose out of his chair and motioned to me.

"I can see that's uncomfortable, Baby. We'd better

head back to the hotel and get you a dry top. Don't want you to get sick."

Vivian rushed over to Dad.

"No, Russell, don't go yet. You haven't had dinner. Jasmine will let Portia borrow a shirt for tonight." She turned to Jasmine. "Get Portia one of your tops!"

"I'm sure she doesn't want to wear my blouses," Jasmine said, not moving an inch, and pouring more gravy on her potatoes.

"We'll go." Dad looked at Vivian. "It's okay. These things happen." He reached for my hand and squeezed it.

"At least, let me fix you both a plate." Vivian looked sadly at Dad. "I'm so sorry, Russell. I've been planning this dinner all day. Even made that meatloaf recipe that you always liked."

"It's a deal. I never could resist your meatloaf, Viv," Dad said. "We'll take it with us."

The doorbell rang. "May I be excused? I'll be back in a sec. My friends are at the door," Jasmine said.

Vivian gave Jasmine a stern look and nodded her head. Jasmine glared at me and left the table.

"Portia, check the linen closet in the hallway, get a towel and dry your shirt as best you can." Vivian stood up.

"Russell, while Portia's doing that, I'll get your food."

"Go get dry, Baby Girl, and then we'll go." Dad grasped my hand.

I hurried out of the kitchen to find the linen closet.

Jasmine won't let me wear one of her old blouses. Good. I don't want to change my top in front of her anyway.

I wiped my shirt as dry as I could, and even though I knew water wouldn't damage my insulin pod, I checked it. I walked over to the kitchen door, which was slightly ajar.

My insulin pod beeped again. I knew my blood sugar was low because I hadn't eaten since lunch. I looked to see if anyone else had heard it, stepped back and closed the door.

Please don't go off again, I begged.

I pulled a piece of candy from my tote bag and quickly gobbled it down. After swallowing the last of the chocolate, I opened the kitchen door just wide enough to hear what Vivian and Dad were saying.

"Jasmine has been getting into a lot of trouble lately. Russell, I had to go to her school a few weeks ago because she was bullying and picking on some kid. Don't have any idea why she's doing these bad things, and she won't listen to me. It's a big problem."

Dad sighed. "We have to find out why she's acting

this way."

All the times we'd talked on the phone, Jasmine never mentioned any problems with her mom or at school.

"There's more. Jasmine's getting failing grades. I had to check to make sure she has enough credits to graduate next summer. She's been hanging out with the wrong kids. About a month ago, she started dressing strangely and wearing a lot of makeup. When I spoke to her about it, she blew up. Just like now—she knows not to leave the table 'til she has finished eating. If I had said 'no,' it would have led to a big argument. So I just gave in to keep the peace. She's rude to my friends—the few I have. I've run out of things to do." Vivian let out a loud breath. "I'm really worried about her, and now she's constantly overeating. She has gained a lot of weight. Oh, Russell, I made a terrible mistake years ago. I shouldn't have listened to my father. I should have told you about her. She needed you in her life, too."

"You're right, Vivian. You should've told me," Dad murmured. "Unfortunately, we can't go back. Jasmine's getting older and starting to rebel. It couldn't have been easy for you caring for her all by yourself. Thank you for what you've done. Let's hope that after she spends time with us, things will get better."

"I pray that they will, Russell. I'm not sure what to do anymore. Thank you so much for taking her. I'll have her all packed and ready when you come in the morning."

Vivian handed Dad a big bag.

I walked into the kitchen. "What should I do with this damp towel?"

Vivian smiled at me. "Just hang it on the back of that chair, dear."

What have I gotten myself into? Do I really want Jasmine to come back with us? She was so nice on the phone. But now she's mean, and she hates me. Will she make my life miserable when we get home?

Chapter Four

The next morning Dad and I tested our blood sugar. No worries for me, because my pod pumped insulin up to three days and nights. But I still had to test. Dad said he didn't like the latest diabetic gadgets and would always give himself insulin the old-fashioned way—using the needle. The New Artificial Pancreas is the latest word in diabetes research. I'm waiting until it's ready—modern technology! It will be great not to have diabetes on the brain 24/7.

Dad and I ate a quick breakfast in the hotel coffee shop and headed to the car. I put my suitcase in the trunk, wondering if Jasmine was still coming home with us. Maybe she told her mother she doesn't like me and wanted to stay home.

One minute she is nice to me and the next minute she is saying cruel things. I'm not sure what to expect.

Jasmine was waiting outside on the stoop of her

apartment building.

Thank goodness. She's coming with us. She doesn't have on much makeup. Maybe Vivian asked her not to overdo it, or she decided to tone it down. She waved and pulled her suitcase down the steps toward us.

"Let me get that for you, Baby Girl," Dad called, jumping out of the car.

I think he wondered if she was still coming with us too.

Did he just call her Baby Girl? That's what he calls me.

Jasmine's mom came out and watched her and Dad put the suitcase in the trunk.

Dad walked over to the stoop and touched Vivian on the shoulder. "Now don't worry about Jasmine. Portia and I will take good care of her."

"I know, Russell. But I'll miss her. Bye, Portia. Bye, Jasmine. Take care and be on your best behavior, sweetheart." Vivian waved. Jasmine waved back. Vivian walked into the apartment building.

Jasmine slumped into the back seat.

"Daddy, sorry about the way I acted yesterday," Jasmine said when Dad got into the car. "And, Portia, I feel bad about your blouse. It was an accident, honest."

Dad smiled and looked at me. I knew he was waiting for me to accept her apology.

I shrugged and forced myself to say, "It's no big deal. I'm okay."

I knew she was lying, but if it made Dad happy I'd accept her apology.

"I *told* Mom you'd say that when she made me promise to apologize," Jasmine said, rolling down the car window.

"Jasmine, have you flown before?" Dad got on the freeway.

"Once, with Mom to San Francisco. I want to sit next to you on the plane, Daddy."

It's not going to be easy getting used to Jasmine calling my dad Daddy.

I looked out the window and listened to her chatter on about nothing—all the way to the airport.

Dad returned the rental car. We checked our bags and about an hour later boarded the plane.

While we were looking for our seats, Jasmine held on to Dad's hand like her life depended on it. She completely ignored me and acted as if *they* were the only two people on the plane. I tagged along behind wondering if maybe she was afraid to fly.

"I'm taking the window seat, Portia. You probably fly all the time," she said, turning around and smirking at me. "Daddy, you sit in the middle between us."

Who made her the boss of everything?

Dad knew I hated sitting on the aisle. I always sat in the middle or by the window because he liked to sit in the aisle seat. He has long legs.

"Well," he said, wrinkling his forehead. "I guess I can do that this time—sit between my two daughters on this trip home."

"Okay," I said with a sigh. "I'll take the outside seat."

What was I supposed to say?

"That's my girl." Dad patted my shoulder and settled into his seat.

"Oh, Portia," Jasmine cooed, "I'm so sorry. I just remembered you told me on the phone that you liked the window seat. Do you want to trade?"

"No," I said, buckling my seat belt. "You sit there."

"You can have it, if you want. I don't want Daddy thinking his baby girl is selfish. When I fly home alone, I can sit by the window."

"No, I'm okay," I said. "Take the seat."

Jasmine smiled, turned to the window and watched as the plane pushed back from the gate.

Dad pulled out a magazine from the seat rack and started to read. I took a book from my backpack and thumbed through it, trying to find my place. I looked over when Jasmine started talking to Dad in a low voice. I could hear her babbling on and on, but it was obvious she didn't want me to hear what she was saying. Dad didn't try to include me either. I guess he didn't want her to think she couldn't talk to him. I tried to read my book, but I was so upset that they left me out that I couldn't concentrate. I closed my eyes and tried to sleep, but couldn't.

It seemed like forever before the stewardess announced that we were landing.

The wheels plunked down, the airplane screeched to a stop, and after a while the door opened.

Jasmine kept talking to Dad on the way to Baggage, even though she'd had him all to herself the whole flight. She never shut up, not even when we were waiting for our bags. I'm sure she planned the whole thing just to make me feel bad.

I knew I was going to have to share Dad, but Jasmine

didn't even know him, and already she was hogging him up.

When we stepped out of the terminal, Mom rushed toward us. She gave Dad a hug and scooped me into her arms.

"Mom," I murmured, holding her close. "I missed you so much."

"And I missed you, too." Mom kissed my forehead and looked over at Jasmine. "Hello, honey. I'm Grace. It's so nice to see you. You're even prettier than your picture. Guess what, your mom called just before I left for the airport. She *was* right. You and Portia look so much alike."

"Mom called already?" Jasmine acted surprised. "She said she'd miss me, but I didn't believe her. She's got her friends. That's all she cares about."

"Oh Jasmine, of course she'll miss you. That's why she called me to check on you." Mom grinned. "Your mom's missing you already, honey."

Jasmine and I slid into the back seat. "You guys have a super OTC car," she said, looking around. She slid her hand over the upholstery and sighed.

"What's that?" Dad called over his shoulder.

"Off the chain. Are you rich, Daddy?"

"I wish," he answered, laughing.

"But you have so much more than Mom and me.

We're poor. We take the bus. I hate it, because I can't ride places in my own car like other kids." She took out the candy bar she had made Daddy buy her at the airport. "Sometimes they tease and call me 'Carless Jazz.'"

Dad laughed. "That's just kids. Don't let them bother you, Jasmine. One day you'll have a car."

Jasmine babbled on and on, complaining and grumbling about how she didn't have anything.

Does she blame us because her mom doesn't have a car? Is she trying to make Dad feel guilty because of what happened years ago? How does Mom feel about what she's saying? Is this what the next three weeks will be like?

Chapter Five

"Is this your house?" Jasmine asked when Dad pulled into our driveway. "It's gigantic. Gosh. You guys live in a mansion! How many bedrooms do you have?"

"Four, and one is yours," I said, praying she'd like being with us.

"NW!" Jasmine said, taking off her seat belt.

"Yes, you have your own room, Jasmine," Dad said, stepping out of the car and opening the door for Mom. "Grace fixed up one of the bedrooms just for you."

Jasmine got out. "Geez, thanks, Grace. What's my room like?"

"Let's take Jasmine to her room." Dad laughed. "Come on everybody, hurry."

Maybe this is what she needs, seeing that we want her to feel like family. She even has her own bedroom.

Mom rushed to unlock the front door.

"OMG! You guys *are* rich. This is just like the model homes Mom and I go to see sometimes."

Mom and Dad smiled.

"Portia, where's my room?"

"I'll show you." I started down the hall past my bedroom to the one Mom fixed especially for her.

"I can't believe it. This room looks like a bedroom in the magazines! There's a phone in here too."

Mom came in behind her and walked over to the bed. "Russell told me your favorite colors were yellow and green." She smoothed the green ruffle on a pillow sham.

"Mom went all out buying green bedspreads, yellow curtains, and bath towels—even some yellow soap. Right, Mom?"

Mom smiled and nodded. She was pleased that Jasmine was so happy.

"Thanks for everything." Jasmine scanned the room. "You guys have all the greatest stuff. You're so lucky."

What does she mean? We invited her here because we want her to get to know us and enjoy our home, not to rub it in. She should know this is all for her.

"Oh, Russell, look at the time. I need to finish dinner. Jasmine, I made one of your favorites, and Portia's too—spaghetti. Your mom told me you could eat it every day." Mom squeezed Jasmine's hand and hurried out of the room.

"I'll get the bags out of the car," Dad said, following Mom down the hall.

Jasmine slowly looked around. "This really is OTC. Your mom spent a lot of money decorating this room and the bathroom. But then, she's rich. She can throw money around." She shook her head and frowned.

"Come on. Give us a chance to show you how much we want you to be part of our family," I said. "Jasmine, I hope you like it here."

"Oh yes, Miss Skinny Minny, Miss Money Bags, Little Rich Girl. You've got everything, nice car, big mansion, lots of money. I'd have that too, but Dad left me and my mother. We were supposed to be his family. Now we have nothing." She threw up her hands.

"I'm sorry you don't have those things, but it's not my fault." I tried to smooth things out.

Dad walked in carrying her suitcase. "Hey, little lady. What do you have in here? This thing is pretty heavy."

She ran over and threw her arms around Dad. "Oh, Daddy, I love you. Thanks for bringing in my bag."

"You're welcome, Baby," he said, ruffling her hair. "I'm so glad you're here."

What is he doing calling her "Baby"? That girl is as mean as a snake when he's not around.

"Unpack if you want," Dad said. "I was told to tell you ladies that dinner will be ready in about thirty minutes. You've got plenty of time."

"Okay, Daddy," I said. "Is my bag in my room?"

He nodded and rubbed my shoulder.

"I'll be finished unpacking by then for sure." Jasmine patted her tummy. "I'm starving."

"Good girl," Dad said, walking out.

"I'm going to go unpack too," I said, before Jasmine started another argument. "See you later."

I dashed to my room, closed my eyes and sighed with relief. That is until I thought of something else—how to make sure Jasmine didn't come in my bathroom and look in the drawer where I kept all my diabetic supplies. Not only was she hateful and a liar, she was probably a snoop too.

No way did I want her to know I have diabetes.

I pulled my diary out of the dresser.

Dear Diary,

I was so happy the end of last summer when Mom and Dad told me about Jasmine. I wanted a sister and couldn't wait for her to come for a visit. Now that we've finally met, she hates me. She calls me names and says mean things to me. I'm confused. One minute she's nice, and the next minute she's nasty.

My parents want me to make her feel welcome. She was really sweet when I talked to her on the phone. We chattered for hours. She seemed like a perfect big sister. But she has changed. Why is she so mean to me? What happened?

—Trying to be nice

I stuck the diary inside a small paper box and hid it in a new place—the bottom drawer under my hair rollers in the bathroom cabinet. This was the safest place I could think of. I could lock my bathroom door when I left the house, and there was no way Jasmine could get in. I knew that because two years ago I accidently left the knob in the locked position when I closed the bathroom door. It locked behind me, and I freaked out. Dad showed me how to use the emergency key that we now keep on the ledge on top of the bathroom doorframe in case it happened again.

It was time for me to remove my old insulin pod and put a new one on. It's pretty easy. I just alternate the sides of my stomach. My diabetic care was so much easier with the pod than the injector pen I used before. I never needed any help now. The only problem was the pod's warning beep. I was afraid it would go off when Jasmine was around. And, if she ever found out I had diabetes, she'd use it against me.

She could never know. I had to come up with a plan.

Chapter Six

Jasmine tapped my shoulder. "What're you doing?" she asked.

I yanked my top down. "Don't sneak up behind me like that. You scared me."

"You took so long and I needed more hangers. What's under your blouse?"

I hurried out of the bathroom, quickly closing the door behind me.

"Just checking something out," I said, heading for my closet to get hangers.

If I told her, she'd have another reason to be mean to me. I can't tell her. I pulled out a handful of hangers and handed them to Jasmine.

"Are these enough?"

"Good job, Miss Slowpoke." Jasmine scanned the room. "OMG! You are so lucky. Look at all the trophies on your desk: one, two, three—eleven and the awards on your wall: First Place, Spelling Bee; Principal's Honor Roll; City-Wide Champion Swim Team Captain. You must be the queen of everything."

She walked to the opened closet door, stepped in and moved my clothes around.

"Boy, look at all these dresses, shoes, pants and tops." She backed out of the closet. "You have everything." She turned and left with a frown on her face.

Thank goodness. She's gone. She hates me even more now.

I closed the bedroom door behind her and took a deep breath.

What can I do?

After I finished unpacking, I went to Jasmine's bedroom, hesitated at the door, and slowly walked in.

She was sitting in the rocking chair. When she noticed me, she looked up and said, "You're spoiled. You don't have to want for anything."

I sighed. "Come on, Jasmine, let's go eat."

She followed me to the kitchen. I could feel her eyes cutting into my back.

Mom was stirring the spaghetti sauce. She looked up

at us and smiled. "Here are my girls. I bet you're ready for dinner."

"Thanks for all the beautiful things in my room," Jasmine said. "I only have a few pieces of furniture in my room at home. Portia is so lucky."

"Yeah," I snapped. "You already told me."

"Portia." Mom gave me *the look*.

Ugh, it made me ill to watch Jasmine being all goody-nice with my parents when she was so hateful to me. If they only knew the things she says to me and the way she treats me when they're not around.

"Your room will always be here, Baby, when you want to come see us," Dad assured her.

There it is again—Dad calling her "Baby." I ground my teeth. At least Dad didn't say anything about me.

I had to find a chance to tell them not to mention I have diabetes.

"When we're done with dinner, Jasmine, do you want to play 'Say It Now,' my new board game?"

I asked her so Mom and Dad would see that I was doing my part in trying to make Jasmine feel at home.

"No, I'm going to my room to call Mom on my new phone."

"Okay. When you finish maybe we can play."

Jasmine had a second helping. She piled spaghetti and sauce on her empty plate. It was even more than she took the first time. She ate more than Dad.

When she finally finished, we washed dishes and went to our bedrooms.

Jasmine likes Mom and Dad. They don't see how she's treating me. Should I tell them? I hate being a tattler. They will just say to give her more time and soon she'll come around.

I read for a while but couldn't concentrate. I put the book down and went to watch TV with my parents.

"Did Jasmine say she likes it here?" Dad asked.

"She loves her room, and she likes you and Mom..."

"I'm glad I decorated the room just for her," Mom cut in. "She seemed thrilled with it. I want her to feel at home."

I hope she appreciates all the trouble you went through to make her room special.

"Mom, Dad, I need your help," I said, looking at them. "Please don't tell Jasmine that I have diabetes. Please."

"Portia," Mom said, "Why not? Honey, I don't see how you can keep it from her."

"In fact, Baby Girl," Dad said, "even if you try and

hide it, sooner or later she'll find out. Why don't you want to tell her?"

"I need to make sure she likes me before I tell her. Sometimes kids don't understand. They're mean, and they say hurtful things if you're different, especially if you have a disease."

"Portia," Mom said. "I think you're being paranoid. You're worrying about nothing. I'm sure Jasmine will understand."

"Maybe, but I'm not ready to tell her yet."

"Not ready to tell me what?" Jasmine barged into the room.

She had changed her blouse and put on makeup.

What's up with that?

"Hey, Jasmine, I've got a present for you," I said, changing the subject. "I'm going to get the necklace I made for you at camp."

Jasmine's eyes opened wide. She stared at me.

I dashed out of the room. No way was I telling her anything tonight.

Before I got the necklace, I went into the bathroom and tested my blood glucose. It was fine. Jasmine has no idea how hard I work to keep my diabetes under control. She thinks I'm rich and have everything. She doesn't know I have to be super careful, or I'll wind up in the hospital.

I turned on my computer, read and answered some emails. I didn't want to hurry back to nosy Jazz. After a few minutes, I decided I was ready to face her again. The necklace was in a small box. I took the top off and held up the bright green string of beads. They were so pretty and shimmered when the light hit them.

I heard Dad's car start. I put the necklace back in the box and hurried to the family room. Mom had curled up on the sofa, watching one of her evening shows. Jasmine was walking into the garage.

"Hey, Jasmine! Where are you going?" I called after her.

She looked over her shoulder at me, grinned and slammed the garage door.

"Mom, where are they going?"

"She told your dad she wanted to see a movie that just came out. He checked the paper, and it's playing downtown. They decided to go. They'll be home by nine with some ice cream for us."

"But, Mom, why didn't they ask me?" My eyes

watered.

"Jasmine said you told her to ask your dad to take her. She said you didn't want to go, and you were going to stay in your room and read. That was nice of you to give her a little alone time with him, dear."

"I didn't say that. I would have gone to the movies. She just wants Daddy all to herself," I ranted. "That's what she did on the plane, all the way home, talking only to Daddy like I wasn't there, never saying anything to me. She's so selfish."

"Portia, don't be overdramatic. This is something new for Jasmine. Let her spend time with him. They need this time together. Try to understand and not overreact."

"But she is leaving me out on purpose."

"Portia, he's *her* father, too. You're going to have to learn to share him. You can't get upset when they are together."

Jasmine planned this. Not only is she a big liar, she's sneaky, too. That's why she changed her shirt and put on makeup. She heard me calling out to her.

"I'm so angry! Why is she doing this to me?"

"Everything is not always about you, Portia. All this is new to Jasmine. She left her home, friends and people she knows. Give her a little time to get used to us, honey."

What can I do to make Mom realize that Jasmine is being mean and hateful to me?

Chapter Seven

"Mom, I'm going to call Grandma," I said, thinking how much I needed to hear her voice.

"Okay, tell her I said hello, and I'll call her later in the week." Mom let out a sigh.

I'm sorry, but I know Jasmine is sneaky and wants you and Dad to think she is so good.

I went to my room, threw the necklace in the top drawer and dialed Grandma's number.

"Hi, Baby," Grandma said. "I wasn't sure if you were back from your trip. How's everything with your new sister? Tell me all about it."

"Grandma, it's not good. I did as you said and tried to welcome her into the family, but it didn't go well. She's a different Jasmine than the girl who talked to me on the phone. She doesn't like me. I can tell by the way she speaks to me."

"What do you mean by that?" Grandma asked.

I didn't want to tell her the whole story, because she would tell Mom and Mom would say I was reading too much into it.

"Jasmine says hurtful things to me when I talk to her."

"What kind of hurtful things, Baby? Tell Grandma what she said."

"I told her that last winter my friends and I went on a weekend ski trip, and I was glad I learned how to ski. She said that's what rich people do, and she didn't want to hear me brag because I had money. She said I wanted to make her feel bad because she doesn't have money. I wasn't bragging."

"Oh, Baby. I'm so sorry. I had so hoped that you two would get along. Did you speak to Russell and Grace about what she's saying to you?"

"No, Daddy thinks spending time with us will help Jasmine, and she's his daughter too. Mom says I'm overreacting. But I know Jasmine's slick and sneaky."

"Portia, Jasmine's going through a hard time." Grandma paused. "You've always had Russell. Jasmine hasn't. It's probably hard for her to get used to this new situation."

"But, Grandma, why does she have to say such cruel things and always want Dad to herself?"

"Remember when I told you to be patient when your parents were having problems? I'm telling you the same thing now with Jasmine. She needs your patience, too, honey. But I don't like her saying things that make you feel sad. That's not good."

"When are you coming for a visit?" Tears rolled down my cheeks. "I want you to come soon."

"I'll be there for Thanksgiving."

"Geez, I don't think I can wait that long."

"Oh yes you can. Are you okay with your new insulin pod?"

"Yes, I love it. At first it was really hard because it wouldn't stick to my skin, so Mom bought a special adhesive tape for me. Then it kept beeping for no reason, and Dad called the company. They said it was defective, and they sent us another one. I know everything about it now. It's amazing. I can even wear it when I swim. I still have to be responsible, check my blood sugar and eat right. But it's a lot easier keeping my blood glucose regulated now."

"You're a smart, mature young lady. I'm so proud of you," Grandma said. "You and Jasmine will work things out. I just know you will. Give me a goodbye kiss. Come on, Baby."

"Mom said she'll call you later this week," I said, feeling calmer.

"I'll probably call her before she calls me."

"Love you, Grandma."

"Love you more, Baby."

The phone went silent.

Grandma expects me to solve this problem with Jasmine. But what can I do? Jasmine hates me, and I'm beginning to wonder why I should even try.

I stayed in my room and played games on the computer. I wasn't going to let Jasmine know I wanted to go with her and Dad.

A little before nine Mom called out, "Portia, Russell and Jasmine are back. They just pulled into the garage. Come see what they brought us."

I went to the den. They'd just walked in, eating ice cream cones and laughing.

"Portia, you missed a great movie." Jasmine wiped her lips with a napkin." Too bad you didn't want to see it."

I threw her a sharp, daggered look.

"Here's your mint chocolate marshmallow ice cream, just for you and your mom." Dad handed me an ice-cold bag. "Why didn't you want to see the movie, Baby Girl? It was funny."

"I never said I didn't." Tears welled up in my eyes. I jammed the bag in the freezer. "I don't even know what movie you're talking about."

"Portia, I asked you if you wanted to go to the movies right after I finished talking to Mom." Jasmine smiled, dragging her tongue over the ice cream. "I really wanted you to go with Daddy and me, but you said no. That was fine because we had a good time without you."

"But you didn't even ask me," I said, shaking with anger.

"Okay, ladies, next time do a better job of communicating," Dad said.

"Yes." Mom looked at both of us. "We're family now, and we don't want anyone to feel left out."

Too late for that.

I bolted to my room.

Chapter Eight

Aaaarh! I was so mad I wanted to scream at Jasmine. How could you be so cruel? What have I done to make you hate me?

Dad came into my room about an hour later.

"Baby Girl," he said, kissing me on the forehead. "Are you okay?"

"I'm so mad at Jasmine. She just wants you all to herself. It's not fair."

"I'm going to talk to her. I had a feeling that you didn't have any idea about the movie. I'm trying to give her a little room to get used to us and to see how we share as a family."

"Daddy, I don't like it when she tells me how poor she is. It makes me feel bad."

"I know, Baby. I'll have a talk with her tomorrow," he promised, rubbing my check. "Night-night."

It took a while before I dropped off to sleep.

Around midnight my insulin pod beeped, warning me that my blood sugar was low. I got up, eased to the kitchen and drank a glass of juice. Then I had to stay awake for a while and test. The next morning I didn't want to get out of bed, and I felt cranky. When I finally dragged myself to the kitchen, Mom and Jasmine were at the table eating breakfast. Dad had gone to work.

"Portia, I'm sorry about last night." Jasmine looked up at me, piling mounds of jelly on her toast. "Daddy talked to me. Next time I'll make sure I understand your answer."

"Yeah, right," I snapped, putting eggs, bacon and a piece of toast on my plate.

She thinks all she has to say is "I'm sorry," and everything will be all right. It doesn't work like that. She has to mean it and stop being so hateful.

Mom passed me the jelly and said, "You two will be living together for the next few weeks. You have to communicate better. Let's not have any more confusion, misunderstandings or hurt feelings."

The phone rang.

"Hello," Mom answered. "Vivian, how are you? Jasmine seems to like it here with us, but I know she told you all that last night when she called you."

Mom frowned and listened. "Uh-huh, I think it was around six-thirty."

She looked over at Jasmine. "Well, she told us she talked to you. Really, she didn't?" She gave Jasmine an 'I'll-talk-to-you-later' look. "I'll give you a call tomorrow. Take care, Vivian." Mom held the phone out to Jasmine. "Your mom wants to speak with you."

"I'll take it in my room."

Jasmine's in trouble. Mom caught her in a big lie. Good.

"Portia, your grandmother and I had a talk early this morning. She told me you didn't tell her too much, just how you feel about Jasmine and what she's been saying to you. I told her you were probably over-thinking what Jasmine was saying. It may be hard for both of you to sort out your feelings, because you've been the only child here, and Jasmine has been the only child in her family, too. It might be difficult for both of you to accept your new roles. And, there's been a lot going on with Jasmine and Vivian lately."

"I heard Daddy and Vivian talking about the problems Jasmine was having in school. How she has changed in the last month. But I didn't think she was going to be mean to me, because we got along so well over the phone."

"Your dad and I are trying not to be too hard on her. We want to give her a cha…"

Jasmine walked back into the room. She glanced at Mom.

Was Mom going to get on her for lying?

"Portia, let's wash the dishes. My time to wash." Jasmine gave Mom a big grin.

Suck-up.

"You both go on. I'll finish cleaning up here," Mom said, "and I'll speak to you later, Jasmine."

Good. Mom's not taken in by Phony Jasmine. Now with Mom and Dad talking to her, she'll have to be nicer to me.

"Grace, can Portia and I go to the mall?" Jasmine asked.

That sounds good. I need to get out of here. "Maybe Caitlin and Maria could meet us there. Is that okay, Mom?"

"What else is there for young ladies to do, but go to the mall?" Mom smiled.

I raced to my room and called my friends. When I came back to the kitchen, Jasmine frowned.

Mom had said something to her about the lie. Yes!

"I called the girls, and they're going to meet us around noon."

"Can I use your computer?" Jasmine asked. "We have time."

After Mom's talk with Jasmine, I hoped that she would do better. Here I go again, giving her another chance. I want her to like me.

"Sure," I said. "Come on, and you can get logged in."

This could be a new start for us. She could use my computer. My friends were great, and I knew she'd like them. I wanted Jasmine to be glad I was her sister.

"Okay, Jasmine, you're on your own."

I went into my bathroom and got my dirty towels, making sure to turn the lock on the doorknob so the door would lock behind me.

"I'm going to put my towels in the washer. I'll be back in a few."

Jasmine got busy on the computer.

I hope she doesn't snoop around in my bedroom.

"How's Jasmine doing on the computer?" Mom asked.

"I think she knows what she's doing. She said she uses the ones in the school's library, and some of her friends let her use theirs."

Jasmine stayed on the computer most of the morning.

Once when I checked on her, she was in front of the mirror putting on lipstick and fussing with her hair. The next two times she was at the computer. I wished she'd hurry and finish. I didn't want her looking through my things.

"Are you ladies ready?" Mom finally called. "It's almost noon."

"Yes, getting the wash out of the dryer and putting it away."

"I'm ready," Jasmine yelled.

She bolted out of my room so fast that she bumped into me in the hall.

"Let's go," she cried.

I threw the wash on the bed, picked up my hand pouch and ran outside. Of course, Jasmine was already in the front seat, grinning.

Mom pulled up to the mall. Caitlin and Maria were sitting on the bench next to the waterfall waiting for us.

"Wait, you two." Mom waved. "Jasmine, hand me my purse, please." Mom gave both of us money.

"Wow! This is 2G2BT!" Jasmine gasped, taking her money from Mom. "Twenty bucks. Thanks."

"Enjoy yourselves, and I expect a call to pick you up around three o'clock," Mom said.

"Okay, Mom," I said, blowing her a kiss. "Thanks."

Caitlin and Maria ran to meet us.

"Caitlin, Maria, this is Jasmine. She's sixteen years old. She'll be here for a few weeks."

"Hi, Jasmine." My friends smiled at her.

"Portia, your sister looks just like you," Caitlin said, looking Jasmine over. "You have the same eye and hair color. Jasmine, Portia has told us a lot about you."

"She couldn't wait until you came for a visit," Maria chimed in.

"Oh boy, you two are DLGs, too." Jasmine smirked.

"What's that?" Maria asked.

"You two are just like Portia, 'Daddy's little girls.' I can tell already."

"Jasmine, please be nice to my friends."

"I'm telling the truth. I bet both of you have your own bedrooms and everything you want."

"So what?" Caitlin crossed her arms. "We're still nice to people."

Here it goes. Jasmine is going to mess up everything.

Chapter Nine

I changed the subject. "Let's go look at nail polish. That's what we came for." Trying to connect with Jasmine, I asked, "What are you going to buy with your money, Jasmine?"

"NOYB," she growled. "It's my money."

"Yes, it's your money," I snapped.

Three of my high-school-age friends called out to me and walked over.

"Hi, Portia," Marlon said. "Who's the new girl?"

"My sister. She's here for a visit."

"Your sister? I didn't know you had a sister. Aren't you going to introduce us?" Nancy asked.

"Jasmine, this is Nancy and Marlon Barnett. They live four houses down from us, and Raymond Vegas lives on Maple, near the high school. They all go to Montgomery High School."

"Hi, Jasmine," they said.

Jasmine smiled. "Hello."

"Do you guys want to go get burgers with us?" Nancy asked. "We're going to eat and hang out at the arcade for a while."

"No, we're looking for nail polish," I said.

"Burgers and arcade sound good to me. I'm going with Nancy and the guys," Jasmine announced. She said to them, "Thanks for saving me from these little kiddies."

"Portia, let's say we meet you back here around two thirty?" Marlon said.

"Good idea," Nancy said. "That'll give us enough time to eat and play games at the arcade."

Mom and Dad trust Nancy. She used to stay with me when they went out.

"Okay." I looked at my watch. It's twelve fifteen now. We'll be back by two thirty and we can call Mom."

Caitlin, Maria and I headed for Rosie's Nail Shop. We loved this place. Rosie would let us try on different nail polish. She had cute little pink tables and seats around the shop.

"Is Jasmine mad at you?" Caitlin asked in a low voice.

"She's been lashing out at me ever since I met her, but

I think she's having problems at home. Grandma said I should be patient with her."

I didn't want to say too many bad things about Jasmine, because I wanted my friends to at least try and like her.

"It's hard to be patient when someone is hateful." Caitlin rolled her eyes. "And that girl is *mean*."

I sighed. "I don't want to talk about it. Let's enjoy our shopping trip. We'll be seeing Jasmine soon enough."

After getting our nails done and buying polish, we stopped by another one of our favorite girlie stores, Little Miss Sally's, to check out some clothes we wanted for school.

"Don't you just love this brown top? It matches David's eyes." Caitlin swooned, holding the blouse next to her. "You two better not tell anyone that I like him."

"Your secret is safe with me," Maria said.

"Me, too," I said. "By the way, don't mention that I have diabetes in front of Jasmine. She teases me enough, and that would be one more thing for her to use. Please."

Caitlin nodded. "We have so many secrets that we've been keeping for each other. We'll never tell."

"Thanks, guys."

"Let's stop by the hotdog stand and get a snack,"

Maria said. "We don't have too much time before we have to get back to the bench."

After we finished eating, we headed for the meeting place. Jasmine had not made it back.

We sat there and waited. After a while, I checked my watch—almost three o'clock. Still no Jasmine. I began to worry.

Nancy and Marlon never get in trouble. What has Jasmine done?

"Do you think you should call your mom?" Maria asked.

"No, I'll wait a little longer. But, Caitlin, call your mom so she can pick you guys up."

Caitlin shrugged. "We'll wait. We don't want to leave you by yourself."

Maria stretched out her arms. "Look at these green and yellow sparkles on my nails. Portia, I love those purple hearts on your thumbs."

We laughed some more at our different, silly nail designs.

Caitlin glanced at her watch. "It's almost three thirty," she said.

Where is Jasmine? I'm getting antsy. Dad will be

home from work soon.

"I'd better call Mom to pick us up, Portia," Caitlin said, pulling her phone out of her purse. "Mom made me promise to call after three hours."

My cell rang. It was Mom.

"What happened? Why didn't you call? Where are you two?"

"We met some other friends, Nancy, Marlon and Raymond. Jasmine went with them for burgers. She said she'd be back before it was time to call you, but they're not back yet."

"Okay, if she's not there by the time your father gets home, I'm coming to pick you two up. Call me if she comes soon." Mom hung up.

We stood looking at each other.

"Where can they be?" Caitlin checked her watch. "They agreed that we would meet them here around two thirty."

We waited for another fifteen minutes or so. No Jasmine.

Where are they?

My phone rang.

"Your father's home. We're on our way," Mom said.

"Mom's coming." I frowned. "With Dad."

Dad's coming was a bad sign. He never wants to leave the house after work.

Caitlin murmured, "My mom's on her way, too."

Just then I heard Raymond shouting, "Boy, you sure can pick'em, Jazz."

"That movie rocked." Marlon pumped his right arm up and down.

"I knew you'd love it."Jasmine squealed. "I've seen it three times. What's up, Portia?"

"Jasmine, Mom and Dad are coming." I clenched my teeth. "You were supposed to meet me back here an hour and a half ago. Where were you?"

"Well, Miss Always Right, if you must know, we saw a spectacular movie after we had burgers and left the arcade."

"We told her she'd be late, but she said your mom wouldn't mind," Nancy said. "Are you in trouble, Portia?"

"I hope not." I wished Dad wasn't coming with Mom.

Caitlin's mom pulled up. The girls got in the car and waved goodbye.

Jasmine smirked and said to her new high school friends, "Don't worry about it, Little Miss Goody-Goody is never in trouble. She'll be fine."

"You'd better stop being so hateful to me," I shouted.

Mom and Dad drove up. "Do you kids need a ride home?" Dad asked Nancy and the guys.

"No," they called out together.

"Okay. Say goodbye to your friends, girls," Dad said.

We got in the car.

"Ladies, how was your visit to the mall?" Dad asked.

I nearly went through the floor. He's always upset when I am late and he has to pick me up, and now he acts like it's okay.

I was so angry at Jasmine I wanted to scream.

But before I could say anything, Jasmine said, "Portia is mad at me because I went off with her older friends."

How can she make up things with a straight face and try to blame everything on me?

Mom said, "Oh, she's not mad. I was hoping you would meet some of the older kids. You're older, and I think Portia understands."

Dad said, "Jasmine, you should have been aware of the time and made sure you were back at the meeting place when you said you would be. You will have to be more careful next time. We'll talk about this later."

Neither Mom nor Dad asked me how I felt, and right

now, being left out made me feel like an unwanted daughter.

Chapter Ten

We rode home in silence. I stared out the window, refusing to look at Jasmine, hugging my side of the car. I couldn't wait to get home.

Dad pulled into the garage.

"You two wash up for dinner," Mom said, getting out of the car. "It'll be ready in ten minutes."

My room was the only place I wanted to be. I wasn't hungry, but Mom would make me eat. I was so angry with Jasmine. She had embarrassed me in front of my friends.

I unlocked the bathroom door, got my diary from the drawer and sat at my desk.

Dear Diary,

I tried to be nice to Jasmine. I introduced her to my friends, but she embarrassed me by calling me awful names in front of them. She showed them how

much she hates me, when they knew I wanted so much
for her to visit us. She's a hard person to like. I don't
think she will ever accept me as her sister. Every time
I'm nice to her, she comes back with something more
hurtful than before. She is trying to make my life
miserable. Is it because she wants Dad all to herself?

—Ready for her to go home

"Portia, we're waiting for you," Mom called.

I put the dairy back in the drawer in my bathroom.

When I walked into the kitchen, Jasmine, Mom and Dad were seated at the table.

I took my seat and slowly started putting small bits of food on my plate.

"What happened at the mall?" Dad looked first at Jasmine and then me. "Portia, I saw you were upset when we left the mall. Tell us what happened."

Dad *never* calls me Portia unless he is very serious.

"I got everyone in trouble," Jasmine jumped in, cooing. "I shouldn't have gone to the movie. It was too long."

There she goes again, trying to weasel out of what she did. Not this time. I lost it.

"Caitlin and Maria couldn't believe you were so

mean," I blurted out.

"You don't like me. You've made that perfectly clear, and you turned your friends against me." Jasmine jumped up and stormed out.

"Daddy, she's trying to make me out the bad guy," I said. "It's not fair."

Dad sighed. "Baby Girl, we understand it's not easy. Jasmine is having a hard time. We're not sure what happened with her and Vivian, but in the last month something has been making Jasmine act out. I know it's not you."

She'd better stop calling me names and being mean to me when you and Mom are not around. Sixteen more days of pain and she will be gone.

Dinner was almost over when Jasmine walked back into the kitchen. She walked over to the table and looked at me.

"Portia, sorry I said those awful things in front of your friends." She lowered her head. "Daddy and Grace, sorry you had to pick us up so late from the mall. Mom said what I did was wrong, but honest, I just wasn't thinking."

There she goes again with those unbelievable apologies. How many more are we supposed to accept?

Jasmine sat down and piled food on her plate. "This

looks good. Thanks for saving some for me."

"Jasmine, we want you and Portia to get along," Dad said. "It's not easy getting used to people you knew nothing about until a year ago. You're my child and I love you. We can make this work if we try our best. We're family."

"I love you, too, Daddy. I'm going to do better." Jasmine got up and gave him a hug.

She smiled at me and Mom. "Sorry. I should've come back on time. It won't happen again. I promise."

Yeah, right. We'll see. I've tried to be nice to Jasmine even though she is mean to me. I introduced her to my friends and let her use my computer when she asks. I don't know what else to do.

"I'm going to take you at your word." Mom sniffed. "You're old enough to make better choices, and in this house we look at what people do, not what they say."

We sat at the table while Jasmine finished her dinner. Dad suggested we play one of his favorite board games, '50 Funny Jokes.' He was trying hard to make us a happy family.

"I love sitting around the table playing games." Jasmine tossed the dice and smiled.

"I love this game. These jokes are really funny," I said.

We cracked each other up when we had to make silly faces and noises to play the game, and Dad was the funniest of all. I felt a little better. When the game was over, Jasmine and I washed dishes and said good night to Mom and Dad.

Jasmine followed as I walked to my room.

"Portia, can I check my emails? I won't take long."

"Mom doesn't let me use the computer after nine o'clock."

"There you go again, Miss Goody-Goody. I just want to check my emails. I'll be quick. Come on, Portia. Your mom doesn't *have* to know."

I closed my eyes and frowned. "Okay, but you'd better be off by the time my bath is over. That gives you thirty minutes."

"Thanks, Little Missy." She touched my arm with a pretend punch.

I hate it when she calls me those names.

I took my stuff into the bathroom and locked the door.

After filling up the tub, I stepped into the pink, strawberry-scented bubbles and let myself sink into the warm water. I shut my eyes, dreaming of Jasmine going home.

My bedroom door slammed. I figured Jasmine had finished her emails and gone into her own room. The water felt so good, I stayed in the tub a little longer. Finally, I got out, dried myself off and got ready for bed.

The next morning, I started to turn on the computer and saw that Jasmine had never turned it off. I opened my email and forty-six messages popped up.

I read Caitlin's first. "Portia, I'll never tell u anything as long as I live. How could u b so cruel?"

What on earth is she talking about?

Dejah's email said, "I told u not to tell NE1. Why did u tell her? U know she would blab 2 EVRE1. Now EVRE1 knows. I H8 u."

What's going on?

Cody's read, "It's your no-longer friend, Cody. Don't ever speak 2 me again, U backstabber."

I bit my bottom lip and kept on reading. By the time I got to email number five, I was steaming. All my friends wrote that I told secrets on them. There was only one way this could have happened.

That sneaky Jasmine read my emails and responded. She told people things others had emailed me, secret things that they didn't want anyone but me to know. Now, my friends think I sent those emails, and they're really mad at me. Thanks to Jasmine, my friends will never trust me again.

What a mess!

I was shaking so hard I could hardly get dressed. I started sobbing and ran to the kitchen to tell Mom.

Jasmine was sitting at the table with Mom like nothing happened.

"How could you?" I shouted, planting my face an inch away from hers. "You are hateful! My friends feel so bad, and they're all mad at me."

"Portia, what's going on?" Mom asked. "What's the matter, honey?"

"Jasmine read my private emails. She sent out secrets my friends told me not to tell. Now they think I did. They'll never believe me again. They hate me." I started sobbing.

"Jasmine, is that true?" Mom said in a stern voice. "Why would you do such a thing?"

"I can prove it," I said, wiping my eyes. "I have the emails she sent while I was taking my bath."

"I was only playing a friendly joke. Why are you making it such a big deal? Your friends are just stupid little girls. Their secrets aren't important." She smirked. "Grace, I don't see why you're so upset either."

"Jasmine, I'm so disappointed in you. That was not a friendly joke. It was a mean, nasty trick. You had no right to do that. No phone calls or leaving the house for the rest of the day. I mean it, young lady. And when your father comes home, we're going to have a serious talk about this. You have gone too far this time."

Jasmine pushed back from the table, slammed her fork down and stormed out of the kitchen.

At least one good thing might come from this. Now that Mom knows what Jasmine's really like, maybe she'll be sent home.

Chapter Eleven

When Dad came home, he and Mom talked for a long time in the kitchen.

I hope she's telling him what happened.

"Portia, Jasmine, come here please," Mom called, after what seemed like forever.

Finally, Mean Jasmine is going to get what she deserves.

I ran to the kitchen before Jasmine could get there.

"Hi, Daddy."

"How's my Baby Girl?"

I hugged him and tightened my squeeze. "Did you hear what happened?"

Jasmine rushed through the door. "I said it was a joke," she yelled, flopping down in a chair. "Can't you and your stupid friends take a little joke? GMAB!"

Dad turned and faced her. "That's enough, Jasmine."

He lifted a finger. "You'll apologize to Portia. Then you're going to email all her friends. Tell them you sent those messages, and apologize. After that you'll be punished for what you've done. One week so…"

"A week!" Jasmine cut in.

Dad frowned. "Seven days. No computer or phone privileges. You can only call your mother."

"But, Daddy, I already told Portia I was sorry. She…"

"No, you didn't," I broke in. "You have all my friends mad at me. You can't get off that easily."

"You're not my mother. So back off." Jasmine swelled up. "Your friends are just rich little spoiled brats. Those secrets are so stupid and silly."

"Settle down, young lady." Dad looked into Jasmine's eyes. "Do you understand what you're to do?"

Jasmine jumped up. "I hate you! I hate all of you. None of you care about me." She glared at Dad. "You never wanted me. So why did you come to get me? Well, I don't want to be here. I'd rather be home with my friends." She poked out her lips and turned her back to him. "Nobody wants me."

"I'm sorry you feel that way, but you're going to

apologize to Portia, and then you're to contact her friends and tell them you sent those emails." Dad's voice kept getting louder. "No phone calls or computers for one week, and that's just to start. You can't go to the concert next Saturday afternoon. I bought eight tickets for you and Portia's friends, but now you can't go. That's your punishment, young lady, and you'll have to live with it."

"Daddy, that's no fair." She sobbed. "I said I was sorry."

"That's not good enough," Dad barked.

"Portia," Jasmine covered her heart with her right hand. "Sorry I was mean to you and your friends."

"I won't forgive you until you email my friends," I said. "And they understand that it was you who told their secrets."

Jasmine walked over to me. "I'll go to your room and fix it right now."

I couldn't believe she thought I would trust her on my computer and decided to keep an eye on her. "Okay, I'm going with you."

"I'll tell everyone that I sent those emails. So they won't be mad at you anymore."

We went to my room. I didn't want to log into my

email, but I did it.

Jasmine thinks she's so smart.

I stood next to the computer. She started typing. After she finished, she asked me to read her message.

I saw where she'd admitted writing the emails and apologized to everyone.

"Now, write, 'Portia didn't tell me your secrets and she didn't know I was tattling. She's innocent. I'm sorry I snooped and read the emails you sent to her and told your secrets. Please email Portia and tell her that you're not mad at her,'" I said.

She added those words. Then she sent the apology to everyone she'd emailed earlier.

"I'm sorry. That was mean of me. Do you think Daddy will let me go with you to the concert?"

I hope not. I don't want you to go.

"That's between you and Daddy," I said. "You'll have to ask him."

"I'm going to see if he'll change his mind, since I've done what he asked me to do." She hurried to the den.

I pulled out my diary.

Dear Diary,

    What is wrong with Jasmine? How can she do so many mean things and think she can get away with them just by saying "I'm sorry?" She is older than I am, but even I know better.

    My friends will not want her to go with us to the concert. I don't want her to go. She will probably embarrass me again. And if she goes, that will give her another chance to do something mean.

    She can't go.

—*Worried*

When I went back to the family room, Jasmine was sulking in a chair. I knew Dad hadn't changed his mind. Once Dad made up his mind, he wouldn't change it. Mom said it was "Tough Love."

"Portia," Jasmine's face lit up. "Let's go to my room and play that new board game Grace bought me."

I sighed. What's she up to? Is she going to start being nice to me? No. She's up to something.

"Okay."

I hope I won't be sorry. I'll just wait for the next prank.

"I have six days to show Daddy I can be good," Jasmine said on the way to her room. "Then he'll change his mind and let me go to the concert."

"Good luck with that." I shrugged. "He's never given in to me."

We had fun playing the board game, 'Famous Actors and Actresses,' and even laughed and made silly jokes.

She was doing this so Dad would let her go to the concert. But she was finally being nice to me and did not call me any names or say mean things to me.

"I'm going to bed. I've had a long day, and I'm tired." I went to my room.

The next day was Sunday, and Jasmine stayed in her room most of the day. I only saw her going to the kitchen to get snacks. Later that afternoon, I went to visit some of my friends.

I still had to smooth things out, because some of them were mad with each other because of the secrets Jasmine shared.

The next couple of days I stayed home, and we played board games and watched TV in her room. She nibbled on candy and cookies the whole time.

I felt a little sorry because she couldn't go to the

movies or to the park with me.

Early on the morning of swim practice, Jasmine knocked on my door. "What are you doing today?"

"I'm going to practice with my swim team."

"Boy, you have everything. I can't swim. Do you think Grace will let me stay and watch the swim team?"

I hope not. I won't enjoy my session. Who knows what stunt you might pull next?

"When Mom and Dad make a decision, they usually stick together, but you can ask her."

"I'm going to see if she'll let me stay with you while you're practicing. It's so boring sitting around here all day, and I can't talk to anyone on the phone except Mom." Jasmine let out a loud groan. "She's not even home most of the time when I call her." She rolled her eyes. "I bet she's out with her friend. She acts like I'm not alive since she met him. She has been going out a lot the past few months. I'm usually home by myself."

Vivian has a man friend, and Jasmine feels left out. Is she jealous of him? Can this be why she's being so mean to me? She thinks Vivian spends too much time with this friend and not enough with her. Is she telling the truth or trying to get my sympathy?

I had to find out more about what was happening with Jasmine.

Chapter Twelve

On the way to the swimming pool, Jasmine asked Mom, "Can I stay with Portia and watch the swim team practice? I've never seen a swim team before. I can't even swim."

"Your dad said you were to come back home and ride back with me to pick Portia up after practice. He said that's the only time you're to leave the house."

I looked at Jasmine and for a millisecond felt sorry for her. She was in big trouble until her punishment ended.

Mom let me out in front of the swimming area.

"Hi, Portia," Rebekah called out. "Where's your sister?"

"She can't leave the house for a week."

"What she did was mean. Is she sorry?"

"She might be, but I don't think so."

"Okay kids, let's get moving," Coach Hill called.

We did fifteen laps around the pool. Then for the next two hours, we practiced and decided what we were going to do to win the swim competition.

Mom and Jasmine picked me up after practice.

"I helped Grace clean her bedroom." Jasmine smiled.

So that's her trick. Do things around the house so that Dad will change his mind. Well, let's see how that works.

"What made you decide to do that?"

"I wanted to help. Have you seen Daddy's red disposable bucket in his bathroom where he puts his used needles and empty insulin vials that he needs for his diabetes?"

My heart fell to the bottom of my stomach.

Did she know? I was sure Mom wouldn't tell, since I'd asked her not to.

"Yes, I've seen it."

I tried to tell Dad to start using the pod, but he wouldn't hear of it. I hope she doesn't guess I have diabetes, too, or ask any more questions.

"I'm going to research diabetes on the Internet so I can learn more about it. I don't want anything to happen to Daddy. I hope I don't get it. Do you know anything about diabetes?"

"Yes. Remember, I live with him."

"From here on, I'm going to be more helpful and considerate." Jasmine gave a cocky grin, "That way Daddy will see that I'm sorry and let me go to the concert."

There she goes, not thinking about anyone but herself. She's still cooking up ideas that'll benefit her.

I headed to my room, tested my blood sugar and cleaned up for lunch.

When I got back to the kitchen, Jasmine had made a cheese sandwich for me.

Did she put poison in it?

"Portia, sit down. Let's eat lunch and talk." She pushed the plate over to me.

She is trying hard to fool Mom and Dad. Usually when I eat my lunch, she was on the phone. This was a new Jasmine.

"How's your cousin, Sarah?" Jasmine looked at me with a serious expression. "Is she coming to visit you this summer?"

"I called her last week, and she was fine. No, she's not coming this summer. She's going to New York to visit family."

"I've never been anywhere. When I grow up I'm

going to travel all over the world—Paris, New York, London, and Hong Kong!"

There she goes, all about herself.

"Let's play a game. What do you want to play?" she asked.

I went along with her.

"Let's go out back and hit the ball over the net for a while. It might be good to go outside and get some fresh air," I said.

She could use a little exercise.

Jasmine groaned. "Never mind, I think I'll help Grace. Maybe tomorrow we can play ball."

There it is, her weak spot. She does not like physical exercise.

"I'm going to see if I can go bike riding with Dejah and Terri."

"I can't ride a bike. Never had one. Never learned how," Jasmine said sadly.

"That's too bad. Riding is good exercise." I went to find Mom.

I needed to get away from Jasmine for a while. She was being too needy, and I didn't trust her. When I rode off, I saw her peeking out the window from behind the curtains.

That afternoon I enjoyed riding my bike around the park with Dejah and Terri. We rode our bikes and stopped to talk with friends.

This is where I want to be. Not at home with Jasmine asking a thousand questions.

About two hours later, Terri said, "Have to go now. Mom said to be home around three. I had a good time."

"Oh! The time went by so fast. I'm not ready to go, but I have to," I said, checking my watch.

"Don't let Jasmine get on your computer again," Dejah teased. "Or you'll be sorry."

"I've learned my lesson. Glad we're friends again. I still have to smooth things out with Rebekah, Cory and Tammy. See you later."

When I got home, Dad and Jasmine were sitting on the patio. I put my bike up.

"I asked Daddy about diabetes, and he was telling me about it. Come and sit with us?"

"Have something to do." I rushed inside before she could say anything else.

Dad, please don't tell Jasmine that I have diabetes.

"Mom, Jasmine is asking Daddy about diabetes. What should I do?"

"Sooner or later you'll have to tell her," Mom said.

"Never. I don't want her to know."

I went to my room, got the emergency key from over the bathroom doorframe and opened the door. I pulled out the diary and sat down on the stool in my bathroom.

Dear Diary,

Jasmine has been asking Daddy about diabetes, and soon she'll start talking about it to me. I'm not ready to tell her.

She has not called me any names for the past few days, but I still don't trust her. I would be so hurt to have her tease me or say something bad about my diabetes. I couldn't stand that. What can I do to? How can I stop her from learning about me?

—Can't tell her

I put the diary back in the drawer.

When I turned around, Jasmine was standing at the bathroom door.

How long has she been watching me? Did she follow me inside? Did she see me get the emergency key from over the door? I have to watch when I come in and out of my bedroom door. She is such a sneak.

She pulled the door to the bathroom wide open and walked in.

"Why didn't you stay and talk with Daddy and me?"

"I was tired and had to do something. We rode for a long time at the park."

She looked at me. "You're hiding something. You've been acting so strange lately. I'm going to find out what it is. Just wait and see."

She rushed out and slammed the bedroom door.

I washed up for dinner and went into the kitchen. I couldn't bring myself to look at Jasmine. As usual she had two helpings of everything.

"After we wash dishes, let's go to my room and play the board game, 'Pressure Cooker,' she said.

"Okay." I wanted to be as nice as possible, because I didn't want her sneaking around in my room in case I forgot to lock my bathroom door. We went to her room and played the new board game three times. It was fun after we learned how to play.

Finally I said, "It's time for me to go to bed. I'm exhausted. I have an eye appointment early tomorrow morning. Good night." I was surprised she didn't try to ask me to see if Mom and Dad would let her come with me.

The next morning Dejah's mother picked me up, because we had an appointment with the same optometrist. I tried not to make any noise, because I didn't want to wake Jasmine. When I got into the car, I looked back and saw her standing at the window with a smirk on her face.

My heart pounded.

Did I lock my bathroom door?

All the while at the doctor's office I tried to remember if I had locked it.

Finally the exams were over, and Dejah's mom took me home. I said thanks, jumped out of the van and ran into the house. I headed for my room. The door was open. I looked toward my bathroom, and that door stood wide open. My heart lurched. I hurried inside and looked in the drawer where I kept my diary. It was gone!

Jasmine stood in my bedroom door with a wide grin on her face. "Looking for this?"

Chapter Thirteen

"What're you doing with my diary? Why were you sneaking in my room? You're already in trouble because of your pranks."

"The other day I was standing at the bathroom door and saw you put something in that drawer." She pointed. "I waited until you left, went back into your room, stepped through the wide open bathroom door, pulled out the drawer, and there it was under your hair rollers!" She held the book over her head, stepping back into the bedroom. "I got a chance to read the last two pages, and now I have proof that you don't like me and want me to go home. You're a spoiled little brat. You have everything, and I have nothing."

I held out my hand. "*Give* it to me."

"No, not until I've read it from start to finish. I can't wait to read what juicy things you've written in your precious little diary."

"I'm going to get Daddy and see about that."

"Okay, take it. Sorry. I was mad at you because you won't help me."

"Snooping around in my room is not the way to get me to help you."

"I promise. I won't read anymore."

Was Jasmine telling the truth that she'd read only the last two pages? Can I believe that she didn't read the parts in my diary about diabetes?

"*Don't* go through my stuff." I was really mad.

"Please don't tell Daddy. He'll never take me off punishment if he knows what I did."

She looked at me with a sad face. I saw tears in her eyes. She left the room.

I had to make sure to lock my bathroom door so she won't search in the other drawers and see my diabetes supplies. Now I needed to find a new hiding place for my diary and the emergency key.

"I only have one more day to convince Daddy to let me go to the concert," Jasmine moaned after breakfast that Friday morning. "Can you think of anything I could do to make him change his mind?"

Jasmine stuck so close to me, I couldn't breathe. It

almost made me wish she wasn't on punishment.

"Nope. Told you when Daddy makes up his mind, he doesn't change it."

"But can't you tell him that you and your friends want me to go, and I've suffered enough?"

My friends and I don't want you to go, and you need to grow up.

"Sorry, Jasmine. He won't listen to me."

"You're just being mean. Your friends don't like me! You spend more time with them than with me. I'm here alone every day."

"It's your own fault. You're the one who spilled those secrets. I can't help it if Daddy said you couldn't leave the house." I looked her in the eyes. "And I don't like being cooped up inside all day. I have friends and want to be with them. So, there's nothing I can do."

"Okay, I won't bug you anymore."

Yeah, right.

I left for my room before she had a chance to change her mind.

An empty shoebox in my clothes closet was the only place I could think of to hide my diary and the key. That would have to do for now.

I turned on my computer and played my favorite game, 'Splashmania.' About half an hour later, Jasmine eased through my door.

Hasn't she ever heard of knocking? What now?

"Sorry I hounded you. It's going to be so lonely here by myself."

"You can watch TV. There's that dance show you said you like, 'Dancing with Ghady and the Gang.'"

"But it's not like being at a live rock concert. Let's go out back and play volleyball."

Jasmine wants to play ball. I can't believe it.

We went outside.

"I've never played before, so you'll have to show me."

"It's easy. I'll hit the ball over the net, and you knock it back. The object is not to let the ball touch the net or the ground. Let's keep it going back and forth as long as we can."

I lifted the ball up and socked it to Jasmine. It fell to the ground.

Jasmine ran and picked it up. "I wasn't ready. Here." She shot the ball back over the net. "Start again."

Most of the time, the ball didn't clear the net, or it fell on the ground. We tried for about fifteen minutes.

At least we were getting exercise.

"I'm tired. Let's take a break." Jasmine flopped down in a patio chair. "Who's going to the concert with you tomorrow?"

"Dejah, Terri, Maria, Caitlin and Aireana. Daddy said Aireana's father and mother have a new motor home and are taking us, so Dad gave her your ticket."

"I wish I could go."

"Come on, let's go inside and play 'Wild Wacky Waves,' the board game Mom bought you." I wanted to get off the subject of the concert.

"Do you think you can teach me how to ride a bike?"

"Yes. One day next week I will teach you."

That answer would have to be good enough for now.

We stayed in Jasmine's room most of the afternoon.

When she was not being mean and calling me names, Jasmine could be fun to be around. I saw some of the old Jasmine that day. She had not called me any names or been mean to me all week.

After dinner, we washed the dishes. Dad asked if we wanted to watch a movie with him and Mom. It was a comedy. I enjoyed it. Even Jasmine chuckled a few times.

"I'm ready for bed." I stood up, not looking at

Jasmine. I was dying to call the girls to see what they were wearing. The concert was the next day.

Dejah and Maria said they were wearing jeans, tops with sequins, and fancy sneakers with glitter on the toes and heels. There were three pairs of jeans I could wear. It was hard to make up my mind. A lot of my shirts would be a perfect match for each pair. I kept looking through my closet trying to find other outfits. Finally, I decided to wait until morning to pick out the right set. I took a shower and checked my blood sugar. It was late when I went to sleep.

That Saturday morning, I woke up late to the smell of bacon. I wanted to make sure I had everything ready before eating breakfast. My diabetes supplies, personal items and cell were in my hand pouch.

I tried on all three pairs of jeans with different tops. It took almost an hour before I decided to wear the jeans with the pink lions' heads engraved on the back pockets. The top that I chose had a lion on the front outlined in sequins. My pink sneakers with green shoestrings were a perfect match.

The clothes that I had taken out of my closet had to be put back. What a mess!

"Portia, come and eat before the food gets cold," Mom called.

"Be there in a sec."

What time is it? Boy, I have to get moving!

I washed my face and hands. I'd take a shower and clean up my room after I'd eaten.

"Good morning." Mom gasped. "Why aren't you dressed? You only have an hour before the Smiths come to pick you up."

"It took so long to decide what to wear. As soon as I finish eating, I'll hang my clothes back in the closet and make the bed. After that, I'll take a shower and get dressed. That shouldn't take too long."

"Your father won't like it if you keep the Smiths waiting. They're doing him a favor taking you kids."

"I won't. Thanks for making my favorite breakfast. The turkey bacon and eggs were good, Mom. Where's Daddy and Jasmine?"

"Your dad went fishing. Jasmine ate earlier with him and said she was going to wash clothes and clean her room today. I guess she wants to keep busy."

"I'm not sure what to say to her."

"You had nothing to do with her getting in trouble. Your dad had to make a decision. She'll be all right."

I went to Jasmine's room. She was busy cleaning.

"Good morning."

"Hi. You're not dressed yet. Better hurry. Have a good time. Wish I could go."

"On my way to get dressed now. It won't take long." I wanted to get away before she started pestering me to see if she could go.

It took longer than I had thought to hang my clothes back in the closet. I hung the outfit I planned to wear on the hook on my closet door. Then I made the bed and took a shower. I was just about ready to put on my clothes when Jasmine called out to me.

What now? I don't have time for you.

"Could you come and show me how to start the washing machine? Grace is outside talking with a neighbor."

"Okay. Let me put on my robe." I hurried to the service porch.

"I know you're in a hurry."

Then why couldn't you wait until Mom came back inside. Are you trying to make me later than I already am?

"Here," I snapped. "The detergent and fabric softener go in first, let the tub fill up with water. Then put your clothes in and close the lid."

"I don't have to push any buttons or turn any knobs to

start the machine, do I?"

"No," I barked. "The machine will start when the lid is closed."

The doorbell rang.

"I'll get it." Jasmine dashed for the door.

Why didn't she stay and start the washing machine? She was trying to make me late.

I hurried to my room. Dejah and the girls burst in. "You're not ready! Your mom said you had your clothes on. Hurry. Let's go. We don't want to be late," Dejah said.

"I would have been ready if I hadn't have to show Jasmine how to start the washer."

Aireana asked, "Is she still up to her old tricks?"

"Yes, she hasn't learned yet, and I fell for another one of her pranks."

I put on my clothes as fast as I could. I didn't want the Smiths waiting for me.

"We're going to have fun today!" Caitlin said.

I said to Terri, "Get my pouch while I put on my socks and shoes."

I looked at the socks and yelled, "Oh no, these are the wrong color."

I ran to my sock drawer and pulled out a mint green

pair. They matched my shoestrings.

"Portia, you have two more minutes, or you won't be going to the concert," Mom called from the front door. "You should have been ready half an hour ago."

I put on my socks and sneakers and checked the mirror to make sure I looked good.

"You look great!" Aireana said.

I grabbed my pouch from Terri, and we headed for the front door.

"Bye, Jasmine," we all yelled.

Mom gave me some money. "You look very nice." She stepped back and eyed me. "Everything matches." She looked at the girls. "All of you look nice. Now go. The Smiths are waiting."

She pushed us out the door. We rushed and got in the motor home. It smelled brand new.

We sat on the long seat in the back and started laughing.

I glanced at the front door. Jasmine stood there watching.

Mr. Smith backed out of our driveway.

A nagging feeling came over me, like I'd forgotten something. Had I lock my bathroom door? I would die if

Jasmine snooped and found my diabetes supplies.

Chapter Fourteen

Things happened so fast this morning and Jasmine tried to spoil my day. I don't remember locking the bathroom door or closing my bedroom door.

Oh crap. No need worrying about it. We're on our way to the concert at the Shoreline Entertainment Center.

The girls chattered away. I couldn't think of anything to say.

"What's wrong with you?" Maria asked.

"I can't remember if I locked my bathroom door."

"Oh, you're worried that Jasmine might go in and look through your things?" Terri asked.

"I saw you close the bedroom door when we left, but can't remember if you locked the bathroom door," Aireana said.

"I can't remember either," I said. "Oh well, it's too late now."

We pulled out our tickets, held them up and shouted, "Here we come, Justin and the Tornadoes. Yeah! Yeah! Yeah!"

When we got to the Center, kids were filling up the place, mostly girls. I waved to a lot of friends from school. Some of them had on 'Justin and the Tornadoes' T-shirts. We were early enough to find good seats six rows from the stage!

I was glad the concert had open seating. I'd known if we came early we would get good seats.

The Smiths told us to find them after the concert. They said they would be sitting in the last row.

Soon the noise grew so loud I couldn't hear my friends. We had to yell at each other. A few minutes later, I looked back and saw a sea of teenagers.

"Hey, I can't wait to see The Rocker Boyz. They're up first." Aireana waved her hand with her ticket stub. "I'm glad your dad gave me this."

"All of us should thank him." Caitlin smiled. "Mom said that was nice of him."

"I feel sorry for Jasmine." Aireana raised her eyebrows and grinned. "But I'm going to *enjoy* this concert."

Boom! Boom! Boom! The drums started. The audience noise stopped. The guys playing the drums played for a few seconds. The Emcee ran on stage and called out, "Ladies and Gentlemen, welcome to the magnificent Shoreline Entertainment Center. Please put your hands together for the fabulous Rocker Boyz."

We jumped to our feet and started clapping. Four teenage boys dressed in black tuxedoes ran on stage. The lead singer took the microphone. He began with one of my favorite songs, "I Just Want to Dance." I knew every word to it and so did everyone else, because we all sang and danced along with the Boyz. Camera flashed. I took pictures on my cell. Kids screamed. After the Rocker Boyz sang their last song, everyone stood up and applauded for nearly two minutes. Then the Emcee came back and thanked the Boyz.

"Next, ladies and gentlemen, for your entertainment," he shouted, "we have a new group whose song is number two on the charts. Give it up for the fantastic Five Poni-Tails!"

The girls danced onto the stage, and the crowd went wild. They had on white cheerleaders' outfits with red boots. Each one of them wore a long ponytail with a red bow holding it in place. They swished their heads, and the music started. "Hear the Song in My Heart" was the song they started with, and all of us leaped to our feet and clapped and sang with them. They danced on the stage, and we danced in the aisles and at our seats. Red, white and blue lights flashed on the stage to the beat of the music.

"This is the best ever!" Maria yelled over the noise.

All of us were singing and dancing. I held up my cell and took snapshots of the Five Poni-Tails.

When I get home, I'll upload the shots to my computer so I can share with my friends and especially with Sarah. She'll love them.

We had been at the Center for an hour or so. Both of the groups had sung three songs, and I had known every word of all of them.

This is so much fun! Too bad Jasmine couldn't come. I hope she's not sneaking in my room.

"Ladies and gentlemen, boys and girls, it's show time! Are you ready for the main attraction?" The Emcee asked. "Ready for the number one group in the world?"

"Yeaaah!" we screamed.

"Well, give a warm welcome to Justin and the Tornadooooes!" The Emcee pointed toward the curtain. A cloud of smoke appeared, and Justin and the Tornadoes ran out.

The Center erupted with screaming, crying and chanting. We were standing, clapping and taking pictures.

"We love you, Justin," the girls sitting next to us yelled. Two girls in the row in front of me sat, rocking back and forth, sobbing.

Justin led five young guys, dressed in white tuxedoes and black top hats, to the front of the stage. The band started, and the group spun around and went into a dance. Justin led with their latest hit, "C'mon Let's Get Started." I snapped my fingers and sang along. Maria and the girls had smiles on their faces as they watched me. They knew I loved Justin and the Tornadoes.

What a concert!

When Justin and the Tornadoes finished singing, the Emcee told us to form three lines if we wanted to take selfies with the performers and get autographs. The lines were long. I started feeling a little woozy. My insulin pod beeped. Not wanting to lose my place in line, I took a candy from my pouch and jammed it in my mouth. In a few minutes I'd need to test my blood sugar. The girls would huddle close to me while I tested. That's what Dejah and I always did when we were in public. It was getting late, and I would have to eat. I hoped my beeper didn't go off again. This is one more thing about diabetes—I have to always be on guard. It never takes a day off.

When we finished taking pictures with all the groups, they gave us autographed pictures. I'm going to put them on my nightstand.

We found the Smiths, and they were smiling. Mrs. Smith said, "I've never seen six such happy little ladies in my life."

"This reminds me of the times when we used to go to rock concerts." Mr. Smith chuckled. "I'm glad Russell asked us to take you. I wouldn't have missed this for the world. We had a good time, too."

All of us piled into the motor home and headed for my house. Then the dreaded thought came back to haunt me. *Has Jasmine been in my room?* I tried to sing and laugh with everyone. Even Mr. and Mrs. Smith were singing. I sang a few words and forced a smile on my face. My head was spinning from thinking about Jasmine going into my bathroom.

Mr. Smith pulled into my driveway. I said, "Thank you so much, Mr. and Mrs. Smith. I had a *great* time." Then I waved goodbye to the girls and said, "Hey, you guys, see you later. I'm starving."

That's funny. Mom's not at the door waiting for me. She always meets me when I go out with friends. And where is Jasmine?

When I stepped out of the motor home, our neighbor, Mrs. Willenbrecht, walked up to me.

"What's wrong? Where's Mom?" Usually when Mrs. Willenbrecht meets me, Mom is involved in an emergency. My heart is pounding.

"Let me speak to the Smiths first, dear." She touched my shoulder and went to the front window of the vehicle. She told the Smiths something while I waited for her on the lawn.

What was going on? I was sure it had something to do with Jasmine.

Mr. Smith slowly backed out of the driveway. The girls waved again.

Mrs. Willenbrecht took my hands. She has always been like a grandmother to me. When my grandmother comes to visit, they spend a lot of time together. She has lived next door to me ever since I can remember.

"Grace had to take Jasmine to the hospital," she said.

Jasmine! I knew it! What's she done now?

"She was out back trying to ride your bike. She ran into an old rusty pipe behind the garage where your dad has that pile of planks and old pipes stored." She hugged me, and stepped back. "Grace and I were standing outside my front door talking. Jasmine made it inside your house and yelled for help. Both of us rushed in, and there she was in the middle of the kitchen standing in a puddle of blood. I called 911 while Grace got a piece of cloth and tied up her leg. Blood all over the place." Mrs. Willenbrecht shook her head.

My cell rang. It was Mom. "Portia, is Helen there with you?"

"Yes, she's telling me what happened. I told Jasmine I would teach her to ride one day next week."

"Well, apparently she couldn't wait. She had to get six stitches and a shot. I called your dad from his fishing trip, and he met us at the hospital. I didn't want to frighten him or Vivian when I called them, but I had to tell them what happened. Have you eaten yet?"

"No, I just got home. Mrs. Willenbrecht was waiting for me, and we're still outside. We're going in."

I unlocked the door, and we went inside. "We're inside, Mom."

"Good. Don't worry about the bloody mess. We'll take care of it when I get home. Eat your dinner. You should be hungry. Jasmine will be all right. We'll be home as soon as we can. Helen said she would stay with you. I'll feel better if she does."

"Okay, Mom."

All the fun at the concert had been overshadowed by this accident.

Jasmine again.

"Portia, you should eat right away." Mrs. Willenbrecht knew Dad and I had diabetes. "That's one thing Grace was worried about before she left for the hospital. She wanted me to make sure you ate when you got home."

"Yes, Mrs. Willenbrecht, but I need to check something first."

I left her in the den and hurried to my room. Drops of blood trailed down the hall. They ran from Jasmine's room, to my room and into the bathroom.

All of the drawers in my bathroom stood open.

My heart dropped all the way to my stomach.

Jasmine knows!

Chapter Fifteen

Jasmine rummaged through all my drawers! Opened bloody wrappers and bandages, cotton balls, Q-tips, testing strips, and drops of blood were scattered over the bathroom floor.

Maybe she was looking for something to stop the bleeding and didn't notice my diabetes supplies.

I went back to the den. Mrs. Willenbrecht sat on the sofa. "Are you okay? Is everything all right?" She adjusted her round, black-rimmed glasses.

"Yes, I wanted to check something before I ate. Let's go to the kitchen. Do you want anything to eat?"

I'll clean up my room later and face Jasmine.

"No, I ate dinner earlier, but I'll take a glass of cold water and sit with you while you eat."

I finished eating and washed my dishes. I didn't want to leave Mrs. Willenbrecht alone, so I suggested we watch television in the den.

"Do you think Jasmine will have to stay in the hospital?" I asked.

"No, I don't think it was that bad," Mrs. Willenbrecht said. "When Grace called, she said Jasmine was getting stitches and a tetanus shot and would be home as soon as possible."

After what seemed like forever, Mom, Dad and Jasmine came home. She had a huge bandage on her thigh. Her right eye was nearly swollen shut, and she had a nasty bruise on her cheek. She had skinned her right arm and the side of her hand. Dad helped her walk.

Jasmine eased down between me and Mrs. Willenbrecht on the sofa.

She had taken a nasty fall. Why couldn't she have waited?

"Portia, your bike is ready for the junk yard. I wanted to surprise you and learn to ride by myself. Didn't realize that it would be so hard to control a bike and that I'd end up like this!"

"I'm glad you're all right. My mountain bike stops quickly at the slightest touch of the brakes. You could've tumbled over on your head and broken your neck. You didn't even have on a helmet."

"I know, but you're so good at swimming, skiing, volleyball, mountain biking and horseback riding—everything, and I don't know how to do anything. I thought it would be easy to learn to ride, and I could surprise you," Jasmine said.

"You should've waited for me," I said. "I told you I would show you how to ride."

"Jasmine has to stay still for at least a week for those stitches and bruises to heal," Dad said. "I don't want her getting any more wild ideas or having to go home with bruises all over her body. Vivian might not want her to come back to visit us."

"That was a fright. Blood everywhere," Mom said. "We heard her calling, but didn't see her. I saw the blood first. My heart skipped a beat. Helen was a lifesaver. I'm glad she kept her wits. Picked up the phone the minute she saw blood and called for help. I have no idea what I would have done without her."

"Jasmine didn't cry. That rusty pipe must have gone deep into her thigh because the blood wouldn't stop until Grace tied her leg." Mrs. Willenbrecht patted Jasmine on the head with a wrinkled hand. "She was very brave. She'll be okay."

"Thank you, Helen, for helping with my other daughter. You've always been there for us. You're the best neighbor." Dad smiled at Mrs. Willenbrecht.

"Russell, you and Grace have treated me like family and even more so since the death of my Oskar. When Portia was born, it was just like having a granddaughter. I enjoyed watching her while you went out, and now that Jasmine is here, she, too, is like a granddaughter."

Jasmine looked at Mrs. Willenbrecht. "Thank you for saying that. I never knew my grandmothers, and I've never met Portia's."

"She's one of the nicest people you'll ever want to meet," Mrs. Willenbrecht said. "You'll fall in love with her, and she'll love you just like she loves Portia." Mrs. Willenbrecht stood up. "I'd better get home. Miss Shaggy misses me when I stay away too long. She's a finicky cat. Good night. Bless you, Jasmine and sweet Portia." Mrs. Willenbrecht hugged Jasmine and me. She smelled like lavender.

Mom walked out with her.

"Jasmine, why did you decide you wanted to learn to ride today? What happened?" I asked.

She looked down at her hands. "I was mad and felt sorry for myself."

Dad said, "Jasmine, I don't want you feeling that way. You're not responsible for what happened with your mom and me before you were born. You're a good person, and so is Portia. I love both of you. You're both special to me."

Jasmine said, "Last year when we talked on the phone, I wanted to meet Portia to see if we acted alike. I know from the pictures that we looked alike. When you said I could come for a visit, I was so happy." Jasmine looked up at Dad.

"My grandfather died when I was fourteen and that hurt me so much. We spent a lot of time together. He was the only family I had besides Mom. He loved me." She stared out the window. "I was lonely and missed him. That's when I asked Mom about you. At first, she didn't want to tell me anything. Finally, she said you had another family, but she would get in touch with you and tell you about me." She sighed. "I didn't think you wanted me. I was glad when you and Portia called and talked to me."

"We loved talking to you and learning about you, too," Dad said.

"A few months ago, Mom began going out with a man

from her job. I felt lonely. I thought she was shutting me out of her life. She's my only family. If Mom left me, I wouldn't have anyone. I got mad and planned to do something about it. I was jealous of the things Portia has." Jasmine shifted in her seat. "I began to blame all of you, especially Portia, for what happened to me and I wanted you to suffer the way I have."

"I wished you'd told me how you felt. It's important that you learn to communicate your feelings to the people who love you. I know sometimes, it's hard," Dad said. "Vivian has done a great job of taking care of you. Now that you're old enough and can take care of yourself, and I'm here for you, she probably wants a little time for herself."

"That's what Mom tells me. She said she had never had any friends, because she wanted to make sure I was taken care of. But I was mean to her because I thought she wanted to get rid of me," Jasmine said. "Since I've been here, I've seen how you and Portia and Grace get along, and I'm sorry for the way I treated Mom. We're family."

"We're your family, too," I cut in.

"I know. On the way to the hospital Grace kept asking if I was okay and kept telling me to stay awake. She held my hand until we got out of the ambulance. My leg didn't hurt so much, because I focused on what she was saying. She never left my side. It reminded me of the way Mom treats me when I'm sick."

Mom came back into the house.

"Jasmine, you've had enough excitement for one day. I think you need to get some rest. After you get settled in, call your mom."

"Okay. My leg's hurting a little," she said, frowning.

"I'll bring an aspirin to your room as soon as your dad and Portia take you there." Mom looked at Dad. "She needs rest."

"Okay, ladies, let's get moving," Dad said.

Jasmine eased up, took my hand and grabbed Dad around the waist. She tried to smile.

"It hurts," she groaned. We all chuckled.

For the next few days, we did everything for Jasmine. Mom said to make her feel "special." She needed a lot of pampering. Even Mrs. Willenbrecht brought her a plate of homemade fudge. Nancy, Marlon and Raymond came to see her. She liked that.

Jasmine loved the attention. I got a little anxious, because the idea of her finding out about my diabetes had returned. She never said or hinted that she knew.

One night about a week later, I wrote;

Dear Diary,

Jasmine hasn't said that she knows I have diabetes. The blood has long since been cleaned from the floors. The bruises have cleared up, the cut has healed and no more swollen eye. She looks and acts like her old self—No name-calling, put downs or makeup. I'll have to get up the nerve to ask Jasmine what she saw in my bathroom. Things are going so well. I'm afraid to bring it up. Should I wait for her to say something about it first?

—Not Sure

When it was time to take Jasmine to have the stitches removed, I went with Mom and Dad. The doctor said the cut had healed, but would leave a scar on her thigh. She limped a little on the right side when she walked. She would be all right when the soreness was completely gone. The color was slowly coming back to the area where she'd skinned her arm and hand.

We stopped on the way home and had lunch at Dad's favorite all-you-can-eat restaurant, Harvey's House. I expected Jasmine to have a hearty appetite, but she only had one helping.

"Eat all you want, Baby," Dad told Jasmine.

She said, "This is enough. I need to stop overeating and use my common sense. That's what Mom would say." She smiled.

I made up my mind.

It was time to ask Jasmine.

Chapter Sixteen

That night Jasmine and I sat in her bedroom watching TV. She looked at me and smiled. "I forgot to ask you about the concert."

"OMG! I forgot to tell you about it and show you the pictures!" I laughed.

Jasmine asked, "How was it? What groups were there?"

"There were three groups, the Rocker Boyz, the Five Poni-Tails, and Justin and the Tornadoes. They sang all their latest songs. Come on. Let's go to my room. I have a lot of pictures on my computer."

I turned on the computer and opened up the file labeled "Shoreline Entertainment Center." Jasmine's eyes were glued to the monitor. She looked at the snapshots over and over.

"I wished I could've been there with you. I can see

you had a good time."

"Yes, I enjoyed all the singing, and I got you an autographed picture of all three groups."

I went to my desk, pulled them out of my drawer, and handed the glossy pictures to her.

Her mouth flew open. "You're the best sister ever. Even after I was so mean, you thought enough to ask them to sign my name on the photos and bring them to me!"

"Jasmine, when you explained to us how you felt, I knew you were sad. I wasn't going to give you the things I had for you. Now I know that the name-calling, bullying and wearing too much makeup was you rebelling because you were hurting and didn't know what to do." I pulled out the box with the necklace and gave it to her. "I want to give you something I made for you while I was at a FriendShip Camp last summer." She opened it, and her left hand flew to her mouth.

"You made this for me? It's beautiful."

"Yes, I was so happy to have a big sister. I wanted to give you something special when we went to get you, but you were so mean that I brought it back home and put it back in my drawer."

She came to me and gave me a long hug. That was the

first time she'd ever touched me like a sister. It left me feeling warm and fuzzy.

"Thank you, Portia. I'll never be mean to you again or call you names. You are my little sister, and I love you." Tears welled up in both of our eyes. We laughed.

"I have one more thing to tell you. If you looked in my drawers in the bathroom or under my shirt," pulling up my blouse and showing her my insulin pod, "You'll know I have to give myself insulin just like Daddy. I didn't want to tell you because I thought you would tease me about it, and that would've been really painful for me."

"Yes, I was being mean and cruel because I didn't understand how to deal with my problems. I'm glad that Daddy and Grace and you helped me."

"I'm glad you realize that we love you."

"When I went in your bathroom to find bandages for the cut on my leg, I saw the test scripts and monitor, but I was so busy looking for something to stop the bleeding that I didn't think anything about all that stuff. I just spaced it off. All this time, you hadn't said you had diabetes, so I didn't think that you had it, too."

"I begged Mom, Dad and my friends not to say anything about my diabetes because I didn't want you to tease me."

Jasmine pulled me into her arms and hugged me again.

"That will never happen," she said, letting me go. "Daddy has told me so much about diabetes, and how he has to deal with it every day. It's not something you can be cured of. I've grown up these past three weeks. You'll never hear me name-calling, bullying or teasing anyone again. I know how to deal with my problems now."

"You'll be leaving day after tomorrow. I don't want you to go."

"I'll miss you, Daddy and Grace, and Mrs. Willenbrecht, but I'll call or write every week, and I'll be back for Christmas. I missed out on presents over the years, and now I want them!" We both laughed.

"Okay, I'll start saving up for all those presents," I mocked.

"I'm looking forward to school in the fall. This will be my last year. I'm going to make good grades like I did in the ninth and tenth grades. I wanted to be an actress—not anymore. I'm going to be a doctor and help people."

I gave her a hug. "That's what I'm going to be, too." We stepped back and high-fived each other.

"Let's go talk to Mom and Daddy," I said.

"Okay. I want to tell Daddy and Grace I love them, too," Jasmine said.

Now I *know* Jasmine likes me. She has accepted me. I'm her baby sister. We are the Maddox Girls!

Acknowledgement

With gratitude to:

- Family and friends, thanks for your encouragement.

- The Society of Children's Book Writers and Illustrators members of the Redondo Beach Writers—Mary Jo Hazard (*The Peacocks of Palos Verdes, Palo's World, P is for Palos Verdes),* Devi Anderson Anton (*The Wish Twister*),and Jalé Pullen ("Mom's Missing Gift") for supporting me throughout this process

- Ms. Travers and Ms. Enriques and their third, fourth and fifth graders at Holy Name Elementary School of Los Angeles, California and to Ms. Shari Hall and her fifth graders at Yukon Elementary School in Torrance, California for letting me share my dream of this book. Your input was well received and appreciated.

- Special thanks to Linda Maher, Elaine Mirsky, and Geralyn Goodman for your support and encouragement.

You are all special to me!

Enjoy Portia's First Unforgettable Journey

ISBN: 978-0-9841650-0-1

"How did everything go so wrong so quickly?" laments the almost 11-year-old narrator of Price's debut novel, after her parents tell her she must learn to administer her own insulin shots rather than rely on them to do it. Young readers follow Portia from one disaster to another as the likable character gains wisdom and strength...Portia's close bond with her caring grandmother adds an affecting note to this overwrought novel. Ages 6–12.

—*Publishers Weekly Select*

No one's life is perfect, and it's dealing with those imperfections that makes us better people. "Portia's Incredible Journey" a novel for children focusing on the constant challenges that young people face through their life, and as Portia's Grandmother puts it, weathering the succession of storms. With a powerful message for youth readers and much to inspire, "Portia's Incredible Journey" is a strong addition for any youth fiction collection.

—*Midwest Book Review*

www.amazon.com www.Barnes&Noble.com
www.elpbooks.net